Beauty
and the Beast
and Other Stories

Look for all the
SCHOLASTIC JUNIOR CLASSICS

SCHOLASTIC JUNIOR CLASSICS

Beauty and the Beast
and Other Stories

Retold by
Sarah Hines Stephens

SCHOLASTIC INC.

New York   Toronto   London   Auckland   Sydney

Mexico City   New Delhi   Hong Kong   Buenos Aires

All rights reserved. Published by Scholastic Inc. SCHOLASTIC and associated logos are trademarks and/or registered trademarks of Scholastic Inc.

ISBN 0-439-43652-4

12 11 10 9 8 7 6 5 4 3 2 1   2 3 4 5 6 7/0
Printed in the U.S.A.   40
First Scholastic printing, September 2002

Contents

Beauty
and the Beast

Retold after
Madame Leprince de Beaumont

Chapter 1

ONCE upon a time there lived a wealthy merchant with three sons and three daughters. Being wise as well as rich, the merchant spared no expense on his children's education. He hired all kinds of tutors. Under their teachers' instruction the merchant's children grew more and more clever.

In addition to being smart, all six children were very good-looking. The youngest daughter was the prettiest of all. When she was small, she was admired so much that people began to call her "the little beauty." As she grew older the name stuck and she became known simply as "Beauty."

Beauty's nickname made her older sisters very jealous. Beauty was not just prettier than her sisters. She was kinder, too. Beauty's sisters' hearts were so full of pride that there was no room in them for kindness.

The older sisters were arrogant. They thought they were better than other people because their father had a lot of money. Even though they were the daughters of a merchant, they would not be seen with other merchants' daughters. They spent most of their time trotting off to parties and balls and gossiping in the park. The rest of their time they spent teasing poor Beauty. They thought it was ridiculous that their youngest sister chose to spend her time reading books!

Because the merchant's daughters were wealthy, many eligible men wanted to marry them. The two eldest daughters stated plainly that they would only marry someone with a fancy title, like a duke or, at the very least, an earl.

When men asked Beauty for her hand in marriage, she politely thanked her suitors. Then she explained to them kindly that she was too young to marry. She wanted to keep her father company for several more years.

And so life in the merchant's house went along fine. Then one day, out of the blue, the merchant came to his children with tears in his eyes. He told them that his entire fortune had been lost. Several of his trading ships had not returned from sea. In order to pay for his losses, the merchant was forced to sell almost all of the family's possessions. They had nothing left except a small estate in the country.

The family had to move to the country house at once, leaving all of their fine things behind. If they worked very hard, like the other peasants in the country, they might be able to get by.

Of course, the two eldest daughters did not want to leave town. They felt certain that their suitors would still marry them, even though they no longer had fortunes to offer. But the girls were sadly mistaken. Their suitors had no interest and no pity.

"Let them act like fine ladies as they milk the cows and mind the dairy," the townspeople said. "The lesson will do them good."

Then, in the same breath, the people of the town would remember the kind merchant, his sons, and especially Beauty.

Beauty's charm and her kindness to everyone, even the poorest people, made her a favorite of all the townspeople. They felt sorry for her misfortune.

Several worthy men offered to marry Beauty, even though she was penniless. But Beauty would not leave her father's side. She had made up her mind that she would go with him to the country to work. Although she had been very sad to hear the awful news about his fortune, she'd dried her eyes quickly. *Tears will not bring back our wealth,* she said to herself. *I must learn to be happy without it.*

When the family arrived in the country, the merchant and his sons set to work farming the land and tending the animals. Beauty kept busy looking after the house. She got up at four in the morning, long before the sun. All day she cleaned and cooked, working like a servant.

At first the work was very difficult. Beauty was not used to such chores. But after a few months she grew accustomed to it and even began to enjoy it. The work made Beauty stronger and healthier. She found that she relished her few moments of leisure more than before. She happily spent them reading, playing the harpsichord, or singing at her spinning wheel.

Beauty's sisters, on the other hand, did not know what to do with themselves. They were terribly bored and slept until ten each morning. They spent their days lying around whining about the beautiful clothes they had lost and the fine company they used to keep.

"Look at our stupid little sister," one said to the other. "She has no taste at all. Beauty is so simple and dull that she is content with this horrible new life."

The good merchant knew better. He saw clearly that his youngest daughter outshone her sisters. He was as impressed by her patience as he was by her hard work and good nature. For not only did Beauty's sisters leave all of the work to her, they never missed a chance to insult their youngest sibling.

Chapter 2

AFTER living for a year in the country, the merchant received some wonderful news. One of his missing ships had, at last, come safely home. The older girls were thrilled when they heard. They hoped that the ship would hold enough riches for them to be able to move back to town and once again enjoy a lavish life.

With his sons' help, the merchant prepared to set out for town. The oldest daughters begged him to bring them dresses, furs, hats, and other finery.

Beauty said nothing. She worried that the ship might not yield enough money to satisfy her sisters' demands.

The merchant noticed Beauty's silence. "You have not asked for anything," he said. "What will you have upon my return, dear Beauty?"

"You are kind to think of me," Beauty replied. After thinking for a moment, she requested a single rose.

In truth, Beauty had no real desire for a rose. She was worried that if she didn't ask for anything, her sisters would be angry with her. They would say she had done it to make them look bad.

So the merchant set out, hopeful that he might fulfill his daughters' requests. When he arrived in town, he was disappointed. His ship and wares were stuck in legal disputes. After long delays, the merchant headed back home even poorer than he had been before.

As he neared home, the merchant began to look forward to seeing his children. He had only thirty miles to go when the poor man got lost passing through a dense forest. A storm grew quickly around him, making it hard to see. The winds blew so strongly that twice the merchant was thrown from his horse.

By the time night fell, the merchant had given up hope. His horse would not carry him and had to be led through the snow drifts. The merchant was sure that before daylight came he would freeze or be eaten by the wolves he heard howling all around him.

Suddenly, through the thick trees, the merchant saw a light. He made his way toward it. As he drew closer he saw that the glow was coming from a huge castle that was lit from top to bottom.

Thanking his luck, the cold merchant hurried into the courtyards. He was surprised to find them deserted.

The merchant's horse, which was as hungry and tired as his master, followed its nose to an open stable. There the grateful beast found hay and oats waiting.

After making sure his horse was comfortable, the merchant walked back to the castle. He went inside and found a large room. There was no one inside, but a crackling fire burned in the hearth. Beside it was a table piled high with food and set for only one person.

Soaked to the skin, the merchant pulled a chair close to the fire. *I'm sure the master or mistress of this house will not mind if I dry myself here. Certainly, someone will be arriving soon,* the merchant commented to himself.

Hours passed and the storm grew louder. Still no one arrived. Unable to resist his hunger, the merchant ate two large helpings of chicken. With trembling hands, he drank several glasses of wine. Then, feeling much bolder, he began to walk around the castle.

Some time past midnight, the merchant came to a room with a fine bed. He was so tired he decided to shut the door and go to sleep. Surely, he thought, his hosts would appear in the morning.

Chapter 3

THE next morning, the merchant woke
up from a sound sleep. He was amazed to
find that the dirty and worn suit he'd hung
over the chair the night before had been
replaced with a fine new one.

"This palace must belong to a good fairy
who has taken pity on me," the merchant
said aloud.

Outside the window, the merchant saw
that the snow was gone. Instead of white
drifts he saw beautiful gardens and flower-
covered arbors. He made his way back to
the room where he'd rested by the fire the
night before. There he found the table set
with a cup of steaming hot chocolate.

"Thank you for your kindness, good

14

fairy. I am grateful that you thought of my breakfast," the merchant said to the air. After drinking his hot chocolate, the merchant left to fetch his horse.

As the merchant walked toward the stable, he passed under an arbor dripping with roses. Remembering Beauty's request, he plucked a stem from a branch heavy with blooms. The moment the flower left the bush, the merchant heard an awful sound and saw an even more terrible sight.

A hideous beast stood before the merchant. The sight of the monster was almost more than the merchant could take, and the poor man nearly fainted.

"Ungrateful wretch!" the beast bellowed in a voice as frightening and horrible as his appearance. "I saved your life. I took you into my castle. And in return for my hospitality, you stole the thing that I love best in all the world — my roses! For this, you will pay dearly."

The merchant dropped to his knees. Wringing his hands, he begged the beast's pardon. "My lord," he cried, "I picked the rose for one of my daughters. I didn't dream I would offend you!"

"Do not call me 'my lord,'" the monster replied. "I do not like false compliments. I think people should say what they mean. I am a beast, and that is what you should call me. Beast."

While the merchant trembled on the ground, Beast went on. "You have daughters, you say? Well, perhaps I could pardon you if one of your daughters would come in your place. But she must come of her own free will."

The merchant's mouth hung open.

"Do not argue with me," Beast growled. "Go! If your daughters all refuse, you must come again in three months' time."

The good merchant swore to ask his daughters and return in three months. He had no intention of sending any of his

16

daughters to die in his place. But he thought he might at least be able to see his children again before his life was ended.

"Wait," Beast stopped the man as he turned to leave. "Go back to the room in which you slept. You will find a large box inside. Fill it with whatever you wish from the castle. Then leave it where it lies and I will send it home for you."

With that, Beast departed.

Reflecting for a moment, the merchant decided that since he was going to die he might at least give his children some comfort. He returned to the castle and found the box just as Beast had said he would. Beside the box were many gold pieces. The merchant quickly filled the box with gold and, just as quickly, left the palace.

Chapter 4

ONLY the night before, the merchant had been overjoyed to find the castle. Now, as he left, his heart was heavy.

The merchant's horse found the way home in just a few hours. His happy children crowded around him, but the sight of them made the merchant burst into tears.

The poor merchant handed Beauty the rose he still held in his hand. "Please take this rose, my Beauty," he said. "The price I must pay for it is dear."

Then he told his family about his terrible adventure. The two eldest daughters were very upset. They cried and pulled their hair. But Beauty did not weep at all.

"Look at her," the sisters said, "her request will be the death of our father. Her wish to be different is his undoing. Yet she does not shed a single tear!"

"Why should I?" Beauty asked. "It would be useless to cry over Father's death, because he is not going to die. The monster agreed to accept a daughter in his place. I will go."

"No, sister!" Beauty's brothers protested. "We will go and kill the beast ourselves, or die trying."

Beauty's father shook his head. "Please, my sons, do not think of facing the beast. His power is so great that I have no hope of escaping." Then he turned to his youngest daughter. "I am touched by the goodness in your heart, Beauty, but I will not allow you to die in my place. I am old. I have had a long life and I will only be missed by you, my dear children."

Still Beauty held fast. "Father, you will not face the beast without me. I am young, but I would rather be eaten by a beast than face losing you."

It was soon clear that arguments were useless. Beauty was determined to follow her father to the palace. Her jealous sisters were secretly delighted.

The merchant was so overcome with the thought of losing Beauty that he forgot all about the box filled with gold. That night, when he went to bed, he was amazed to find it sitting in his room. The merchant was rich once more, but he did not tell his children. He knew they would want to return to town and he had decided to live out his life in the country. He told his secret to only one other living soul: Beauty.

Beauty was thrilled to hear about the newfound wealth. She told her father that while he was away, two of her sisters' suitors had come to visit. Even though they had been nothing but cruel to her, Beauty loved her sisters with all her heart and wished them well. She was delighted when her father agreed to use his new-found fortune to give the older girls the lavish weddings they dreamed of.

Chapter 5

THREE months passed quickly. Soon it was time for the merchant to return to the beast's castle. When Beauty and her father set off, the older sisters rubbed their eyes with an onion so it would look as though they were crying. Beauty's brothers cried real tears, and so did her father. Only Beauty kept a dry eye, for she did not wish to add to her family's sorrow.

The horse knew the way to the beast's castle. By evening, Beauty and her father could see it clearly, lit up in the distance. As before, the stable was ready with oats and hay for the horse. And as before, the great hall held a table heaped with food. But this time the table was set for two people.

When she saw the food, Beauty thought to herself, *The beast must want to fatten me up before he eats me.* But she did her best to appear cheerful and calm. Beauty served her father and sat down to eat, though neither of them had much of an appetite.

Just as soon as they were finished, Beauty and her father heard a terrible noise. Beast was coming. The merchant, with his eyes full of tears, prepared to say good-bye to his daughter. Beauty sat trembling. The castle walls shook as Beast thundered down the hall.

When Beast stood before them, Beauty was shocked by his appearance. He was truly horrible to look at.

"Did you come willingly?" Beast asked the girl in his awful voice.

"Ye-e-es," Beauty replied, summoning as much courage as she could.

"You are very good, and I am very grateful," Beast bowed to Beauty. Then he turned to the merchant. "You are an honest man. Tomorrow morning you will be on your way. Do not think of coming back here again." With that, Beast disappeared, leaving Beauty alone with her father.

"Daughter," the merchant cried as he embraced Beauty, "I am nearly dead of fright already. You must go home and leave me here to die."

"No, Father," Beauty said firmly. "Tomorrow morning you are the one who must go. I feel that heaven may have mercy on me."

When Beauty and the merchant went to their beds that night, they did not expect to be able to sleep a wink. Yet the moment their heads touched the pillows, their eyes closed and they slept deeply.

A lady appeared in Beauty's dreams. "Your fine character has made me very happy, Beauty," the lady said. "And your kind deed, giving up your own life to save your father, is an act of goodness that will not go unrewarded."

24

When she awoke, Beauty told her father about the dream. The merchant was comforted. Still, he could not help sobbing loudly when the time came to say good-bye to his beloved child.

Beauty did her best to be brave, but after her father had gone she sat down in the great hall and began to cry. Then she remembered the promise the lady in her dream had made. Beauty found her courage once again and dried her eyes.

I have only a short time to live, Beauty thought, *I will not waste it grieving. Soon the beast will devour me. Until then, I will admire the splendor that surrounds me.*

Beauty got up from her seat and began to explore the castle. She had not gone far when she came upon a room with a sign on the door. The sign read, BEAUTY'S ROOM. Beauty pushed open the door and was dazzled by what she saw within.

The room was filled with magnificent furniture. There was a fine bed and couches, shelves and shelves of books, a harpsichord, and volumes of music.

"Well, I certainly won't be bored," Beauty murmured to herself. A moment later, she had another thought. *Surely such wonderful things would not have been left for me if I were only going to spend one day here.* This idea gave Beauty fresh hope. Soon she was actually enjoying herself. As she looked over the bookcase, she came upon a book unlike the others. Inside, written in gold letters, was a message.

Welcome, Beauty, do not fear
You shall be our mistress here.
Speak your wishes to the air
All you want will soon appear.

Beauty sighed. "The only thing I want is to see my father again and know that he is all right."

As soon as Beauty finished speaking, she spotted a large mirror. In the reflection was her own home! She watched as her father approached the house. He rode slumped over in the saddle, and Beauty could tell he had been crying. It made her heart ache to see her father so upset. When her sisters came out to meet him, he sat up straighter and tried to smile. The sisters pretended to be sad that Beauty had not returned. But behind their fake frowns were smiles of satisfaction.

After a moment the vision faded. Beauty's heart was heavy, but she was grateful to have glimpsed her father and family. To see them again was a special gift. The giver of such a gift could not be horrible and cruel.

Perhaps the beast is a good beast, Beauty thought. *Perhaps he means me no harm.*

Chapter 6

AT lunchtime Beauty returned to the
great hall. Once again she found the table
set with fine dishes and delicious food.
While she ate, Beauty was entertained by
a wonderful concert performed by invisi-
ble musicians.

At dinner Beauty thought she would eat
alone again. But just as she sat down she
heard Beast's terrible roar. Even though
she knew she had nothing to fear, Beauty
could not help feeling terrified when
Beast entered the room.

"Good evening, Beauty," Beast greeted
her. "Will you please allow me to watch
you while you dine?"

"As you wish," Beauty replied. "You are the master of this house."

"That is not so," Beast replied. "You are the mistress now. I am but your servant. If you would like me to go, if my presence troubles you, you have only to say so. I will go. Don't you find me very ugly?"

"Yes," Beauty answered. "I will tell you honestly. I do find you ugly, but I also believe that you are kind."

Beast bowed his head. "Eat well, Beauty, and be happy in your new home. Everything here is yours. My only concern is your happiness."

"You are very generous," Beauty said, bowing in return. "You have provided me every comfort. What pleases me most is your kind heart. When I think of that you hardly seem ugly at all."

Beast nodded humbly. "It may be true that I have a good heart. Still, I am a beast."

"There are many men that act more like beasts than you do," Beauty said. "I would choose you and your monstrous form over a man with a cruel, ungrateful, or corrupt heart."

"I wish that I could pay you such a pretty compliment in return," Beast said. "But I am so slow-witted that all I can say is thank you."

Beauty ate well while she talked with the beast. Her fear was nearly gone. She was beginning to feel relaxed when Beast asked a terrifying question.

"Beauty, will you be my wife?"

For a long time Beauty did not dare answer. She did not want to make Beast angry by refusing. At last she replied in a shaky voice. "No, Beast."

Poor Beast let out a sigh so heavy that it whistled through the castle like the wind before a storm, and stood to leave. On his way out, he turned several times to gaze mournfully at Beauty.

Beauty was relieved to see Beast go, but his sadness moved her. *It is a pity he is so ugly,* Beauty thought, *for his heart is so good.*

Chapter 7

THREE months passed peacefully. Beauty spent her days reading, playing the harpsichord, and walking in the rose gardens. In the evenings Beast visited her. The two would talk over dinner, and though Beast was not as clever as some, he had good common sense. At almost every visit Beauty discovered something new and likable about him. Instead of dreading his visits, Beauty found herself looking forward to Beast's company. She often checked the clock to see if it was close to the hour when Beast always appeared.

Only one thing about Beast's visits bothered Beauty. Every night before he left the great hall, Beast asked Beauty to be his wife. Every night, Beauty refused. And every night, Beast departed, looking so downcast that at last Beauty decided to say something more.

"Dear Beast," she told him. "I wish that I could tell you I would marry you. But I am too honest to fool you or allow you to think that I could ever be your bride. Please, try to be happy knowing that I am your friend."

"I am afraid that I must be happy with that," Beast said. "I know all too well that I am a terrible monster. Yet I cannot help but love you with all my heart. If you will only promise to stay here with me forever, then I shall be happy."

Beauty's cheeks flushed. She had seen her father in the mirror recently. He was grief-stricken and wasting away without her. She wanted to see him again very badly.

"I could stay with you here forever,"

Beauty said, "except for one thing. I have such a longing to see my father that I cannot be happy knowing I will never see him again."

"I can't allow you to suffer," Beast replied sadly. "I will send you back to your father. You shall stay with him, and your poor Beast will waste away without you."

"No," Beauty cried. "I care for you too much to cause you pain. But I have seen in the mirror that my sisters are married and my brothers joined the army. My father is all alone. Please let me stay with him just for one week. If you let me go, I promise I will return to you."

"Very well," Beast said solemnly. "When you wake tomorrow morning you will be home. But remember your promise. When you are ready to come back, lay your ring on the table before you go to sleep. Farewell, Beauty." The beast sighed as he said good-bye, and Beauty went to bed feeling sad that she had hurt him.

When Beauty woke up the next morning she was at her father's house, just as Beast had promised. She rang a bell that was next to her bed and the maid who answered it screamed at the sight of her. Beauty's father rushed upstairs to see what the noise was about and nearly died of happiness when he saw his dear daughter. The startled merchant hugged Beauty and could not let her go.

When Beauty's father finally did release her, Beauty hurried to change out of her nightclothes. *Oh, dear,* Beauty thought. She had not brought other clothes to put on. But the maid told Beauty that a whole chest of clothes had appeared in the next room. It was filled with dresses trimmed in gold and diamonds.

Beauty was touched that Beast had thought to send her clothes. She chose the simplest gown, then asked the maid to wrap up the others. She wanted to give them to her sisters as a present. No sooner were the words out of her mouth than the chest disappeared.

"Perhaps," Beauty's father said, "Beast would like you to keep the gowns for yourself." At that moment, the chest of dresses appeared again where it had been before.

While Beauty dressed, her sisters and their husbands were invited to the house for a visit. Beauty was eager to see them. She soon discovered that, even though they had married, they were still very unhappy.

The eldest sister had married an extremely handsome man. He was so good-looking that his appearance was all he ever thought about. He admired himself from morning to night. He was so busy thinking about his looks that he completely neglected his wife.

The second sister married a clever man. But this man only used his wit to insult others, and he insulted his wife more than anyone else.

When the two sisters saw Beauty, lovely as ever and dressed like a princess, they grew sick with envy. Beauty hugged them and treated them sweetly. But the sisters could not hide their jealousy. When Beauty told them how happy she was living in the castle with Beast, the sisters became even more jealous.

Finally the sisters could not take it any longer. They went out in the garden to complain to each other.

"Why should that brat be happier than we are?" they asked each other. "Is she so much better than us?"

"I have an idea," the eldest sister said. "Let's persuade Beauty to stay longer than a week. Maybe when her silly Beast finds she has broken her promise, he will be so angry that he will devour her at last."

"We must be very sweet to her," the

other sister said. "That way she will not suspect our plan."

The two sisters agreed to the trick, then went back inside. They were so nice to Beauty that the youngest sister wept tears of joy.

When the week had passed, Beauty's sisters begged her to stay. When she talked of leaving, they sobbed and tore their hair out. Beauty hated to see her sisters so upset, so she agreed to stay a week longer.

Chapter 8

ALTHOUGH Beauty stayed with her family, she could not help but worry about Beast. She felt terrible for breaking her promise and worried that her absence would cause him pain. Most of all she missed him terribly, for she had truly grown to care for him.

On the tenth night in her father's house, Beauty dreamed that she was in the castle garden. There she saw Beast lying flat upon the grass. He was near death, and in a weakened voice he asked Beauty why she had forgotten her promise to return to him. Beauty woke suddenly and burst into tears.

"Oh, how wicked I have been," Beauty

cried. "I am cruel to cause Beast so much grief when he has shown me nothing but kindness! He has done all he can to make me happy. It is not his fault that he is ugly and slow-witted. His goodness alone is more than enough. Why did I refuse to marry him? Surely I would be happier with him than either of my sisters are with their husbands. It is neither wit nor appearance that makes a good husband. It is good character, virtue, and kindness — all qualities that Beast possesses. He has my respect, my friendship, my gratitude, and my heart. It is wrong of me to hurt him so, and if I continue to make him miserable I shall regret it all my life."

Beauty stood and placed her ring on the table, just as Beast had instructed. She quickly returned to bed and fell fast asleep.

When Beauty awoke she was overjoyed to find herself in the beast's castle. Beauty dressed in her finest gown. She tried to be patient, but felt she would die waiting for the hour of Beast's visit to come.

Beauty paced the halls. She picked up her books and put them down again unread. She tried to play the harpsichord but was too distracted. At last the clock chimed and Beauty sat down to dinner. But Beast did not appear.

Beauty's heartbeat quickened. Worried that her absence had caused Beast's death, she ran through the castle calling for him. Beauty searched everywhere. At last she remembered her dream and dashed out to the garden.

Beast lay unmoving on the grass. Beauty was sure he was dead. She threw herself across him and placed her head on his chest. When she heard his heart beating she hurried to the canal for water.

As soon as the water touched Beast's face, he opened his eyes. "You forgot your promise," he said. "I was so sad to have lost you. I've been very sick. Now that you have returned I can die happy. I have had the pleasure of seeing you once more."

"No, dear Beast, you must not die!" Beauty said. "Live and be my husband. From this moment on, I give you my hand and swear to be yours. I thought that I felt only friendship for you, but my fear at nearly losing you has convinced me that I cannot live without you."

The moment those words were out of Beauty's mouth the castle lit up with sparkling lights. Fireworks and music filled the air.

Startled, Beauty looked away from her Beast for only a moment. When she turned back, the most handsome prince ever seen was in his place.

Beauty was unable to tear her gaze away from his. "Where has Beast gone?" she asked, looking into the prince's eyes.

"You see him before you," the prince answered. "A wicked fairy put a spell on me.

I was forced to keep a beast's form until a worthy girl agreed to marry me. I was not allowed to show my true appearance or my intelligence until she learned to love me without them. You alone saw past my form and simplicity to the goodness of my heart. I offer you my crown."

Beauty was stunned. She held out her hand to the prince and together they went inside his castle. There Beauty was astonished to find her father and siblings standing in the great hall. Standing with them was the lady who had appeared to Beauty in her dream.

The lady kissed the prince on his forehead.

"At last my wicked sister's spell is broken," she said. "I did my best to soften the curse. Though I could not reverse it, I *could* help to lure a worthy girl to the castle." Then the magical lady looked at Beauty.

"Beauty," the lady said softly, "come and receive your reward. Because you chose merit over beauty or wit, you deserve to have all of those qualities combined in one person. It is your destiny to become a great queen. I trust the throne will not spoil you or let you forget yourself."

Then the lady turned to Beauty's sisters. "As for you," she said, "you shall both be turned to statues. Beneath your stone encasements you will continue to think and feel. For I can think of no better punishment than for you to stand at Beauty's door and witness her happiness. If you come to recognize your faults, you may return to your present forms, though I am afraid that you will remain statues forever. Pride, anger, greed, and laziness are faults that can be corrected. But only a miracle can cure a cruel and envious heart."

With a flick of her wand, the lady transported everything in the hall to the prince's kingdom. There, the prince's subjects rejoiced at his return. The celebration lasted for weeks and at the end of it Beauty and the prince were married.

Beauty and her prince lived for many years in happiness — a happiness made complete because it was founded on goodness.

The Lady
and the Lion

Retold after
The Brothers Grimm

ONCE there was a man with three daughters. The man loved his daughters, but his business required him to travel quite often. One day, as he prepared for a long journey, he asked his children what they would like him to bring home for them.

"Pearls," said the first.

"Diamonds," said the second.

"Please, dear father," said the third, "I would like nothing better than a lark singing on the wing."

"Very well," their father answered. "If that is what you want, that is what you will have." He kissed each of the girls and set off.

The man did not have to go far to find the diamonds and pearls that his first two daughters requested. He was able to buy them easily. But the lark was harder. He searched everywhere without luck and was beginning to worry. He did not want to disappoint his youngest and favorite child.

One day, as the man's journey was nearing an end, he passed through a large wood. In the middle of the wood he saw a splendid castle. Nearby stood a tall tree. And on the top of the tree the man saw a singing lark!

"Ah, I have found you in the nick of time!" the man said to the lark. Then he sent his servant to capture the bird. But no sooner had the servant gotten down from his horse and approached the tree than a lion appeared.

"Who dares to steal my lark?" the lion growled. "I will eat any thief who tries."

"My apologies," the traveler said, stepping between his servant and the great cat. "I did not know the bird was yours. I will do anything to repay my offense, but please spare my life."

The lion paced around the man. "The only thing that might save you is this," he growled. "Promise that you will send me whatever greets you first when you arrive home. If you promise me that, I will give you both your life and the bird."

The man hesitated. "But what if I am met by my youngest and favorite daughter? She often runs to meet me when I arrive."

"You might just as easily be greeted by a cat or dog," the man's nervous servant pointed out.

Because the traveler wanted very much to see his children again, he let the servant persuade him. With the lark in hand he promised the lion what was asked and set out for home.

Just as he feared, when the man reached his house and opened the door it was his youngest daughter who greeted him first. She ran to him and covered him in hugs and kisses. When she saw the singing lark she was overjoyed. The poor girl's father could not share in his daughter's happiness. As he watched her dance around him he began to cry.

"My dear child, this lark has cost me more than you know," the man wept. "To get it I had to promise you to a lion." Between sobs he told his daughter all that had happened.

When the tale was finished, the daughter comforted her father as best she could. "I will keep your promise," she said.

"I fear the lion will tear you to pieces when you are under his power," the father wailed. He begged his daughter not to go.

"I will go and soften the lion's heart," she replied. "Then I will return to you, safe and sound."

In the morning, the youngest daughter

said good-bye and strode confidently into the woods. Soon several lions surrounded her and escorted her to a grand castle. There she found that the lion who owned the lark was not really a lion at all. He was an enchanted prince.

The prince and all of his royal subjects had been put under a spell. By day they were lions, but by night they resumed their human form.

The lion prince was so charming that the traveler's daughter fell deeply in love with him and soon the two were married.

They lived their lives happily, sleeping during the day and staying up at night. Then one evening, the lion prince came to his wife and said, "Tomorrow your oldest sister is getting married at your father's house. If you would like to join the celebration my lions will escort you."

The girl was anxious to see her family again, especially her father. She had grown from a girl to a lady in the time since she had left and had so much to tell them. So the next day, the lady left the castle in the company of the prince's royal lions.

When she arrived home, the lady's family was overjoyed. She had been gone so long that they all thought she was dead, torn to shreds by the lion's claws. They were happy to learn that she was alive and well, and thrilled that she had married the fearsome lion who was really a wonderful prince.

The lady stayed with her family as long as the wedding festivities lasted. Then she bid them good-bye and went back into the woods.

When the time came for her second sister to marry, the lady went to her husband. "This time you must come with me," she said.

"It would be too dangerous," the lion prince replied. "I am safe in my kingdom, but if even a flicker of light touches me during the night I will be changed to a dove and have to fly about for seven years."

"If you will only go with me I will protect you," the lady promised. "I will keep off every spark of light. Not a ray or gleam will touch you."

So the lady and her prince went to the wedding. They even took along their young child.

To protect her husband, a great hall was built at the lady's family home. It had thick walls, so that no light could sneak in. At night, when the wedding torches were lit, the lion prince could stay safe within the walls. But the door to the hall was made with wood that had not dried completely. And when the wood dried, the door split, making a tiny crack that no one noticed.

The wedding celebration itself was splendid. After the ceremony, the whole wedding party left the church, carrying lights and torches. As they passed by the lion's hall, a ray no bigger than a strand of hair shone through the cracked door and fell upon the prince. The moment the ray touched him, the prince was changed.

When the prince's wife came to look for him, she saw in his place a white dove.

"For seven years I must fly without stopping," the dove said. "Every seventh step I will release a feather and a drop of blood to show you where I have gone. Follow the path and you might free me."

As soon as he had spoken, the dove flew out the door. The lady followed. Just as the dove had promised, it let fall a drop of blood and a feather every seventh step. And the lady was able to find it and follow wherever it flew.

In that way the lady wandered the world, never resting. When nearly seven years had passed, the lady felt her spirits lifting. She thought she would soon be reunited with her husband. But the lady's troubles were far from over.

The next day the feather and the drop of blood did not fall. The lady searched the skies, but the dove had vanished.

The lady sank to her knees. She did not know what to do. *There is no man who can help me now,* she thought. Instead she decided to ask the sun.

After climbing as high as she could, the lady called out loudly. "Sun, you shine each day on all of the mountains and valleys of the world. Have you seen a white dove fly by?"

"No," the sun answered. "I have not seen a dove. But take this little box on your search. Open it when you are in dire need."

The lady thanked the sun and took the box.

Soon night fell and the moon shone. *Perhaps the moon can help me,* the lady thought. And she called out, "Moon, you shine all night on all of the forests and fields. Have you seen a white dove fly by?"

"No," the moon answered. "I have not seen a dove. But here is an egg. Break it when you are in dire need."

The lady thanked the moon and took the egg.

Soon the north wind began to blow. *Perhaps the north wind can help me*," the lady thought. Once more the lady called out, "North wind, you blow through all of the trees and leaves. Have you seen a white dove fly by?"

"No," the north wind answered. "I have not seen a dove. But I will ask the other winds. Perhaps one of them has seen it."

The north wind asked the east and the west winds. Neither of them had seen the dove. Then he asked the south wind.

"I have seen a dove," the south wind said. "It flew to the Red Sea and turned into a lion. It is there now, locked in a battle with an enchanted dragon."

The north wind carried this news back to the lady. "Go to the Red Sea," the north wind told her. "There you must pick the eleventh reed that is growing on the right bank. Use the reed to strike the dragon. If you succeed, both the lion and the dragon will regain their true human shapes.

"But beware, for the dragon is really an evil princess. As soon as the lion has turned into a man you must find the winged griffin. Leap upon his back with your true love and the griffin will carry you across the sea."

The lady thanked the north wind and turned to go.

"That is not all," said the north wind. "Here is a nut. When you come to the middle of the ocean, drop this nut into the sea. It will grow quickly into a tree, reaching out of the water. Let the griffin rest on the tree. If it is not allowed to rest, the griffin will not be strong enough to carry you across the sea."

The lady took the nut and traveled to the Red Sea. She did just as she was told. She cut the eleventh reed and struck the dragon with it. Just as the winds had said, the dragon and lion turned into a princess and prince. But before the lady could take her true love's hand, the princess grabbed the prince and rode off with him on the back of the griffin.

The weary lady felt as if her heart would break. She sat down on the ground and cried. She had come too far and too long to give up now. At last she found her courage. "Wherever the winds blow and as long as the cock crows I will search for my love."

She continued her journey until she came to the castle where the prince and princess were living. As she approached, she heard there was to be a wedding celebration. The prince and the princess were to be married!

Heaven help me, the lady said to herself. Then she opened the box the sun had given her. Inside was a gown as brilliant as the sun itself. She put it on and went to the castle.

Everyone in the castle, including the princess, could not take their eyes off the dress. The princess liked the dress so much she asked the lady if she could buy it from her.

"You may buy it," the lady answered, "but not with goods or gold. Only flesh and blood."

"What do you mean?" the princess asked.

"You may have the dress only if I am allowed to speak to the prince tonight in his chamber."

At first the princess refused. Then, gazing once more at the dress, she agreed.

When night fell, the lady was taken to the prince's room. The prince lay sleeping as the lady spoke. "For seven years I have followed you. I have been to the sun and the moon and the four winds. I have even helped you fight the dragon. Please say you have not forgotten me."

The prince said nothing. He slept so soundly that he thought the lady's voice was just a rustling breeze.

No matter what she did, the poor lady could not wake him. She did not know that the princess had asked her servant to give the prince a sleeping potion.

When morning came the lady was forced to give the princess her dress. She was so upset that she ran from the castle and threw herself down in a meadow. The poor lady was beginning to cry when she remembered the egg the moon had given her.

The lady cracked the egg and out popped a golden hen and twelve gilded chicks. The little chicks chirped and scurried about.

Filled with hope, the lady sprang up and chased the chickens all over the meadow. From her window, the princess saw the golden chicks. They were so pretty that the princess wanted them for herself and asked the lady if they were for sale.

"You may buy them," the lady answered, "but not with goods or gold. Only flesh and blood. Let me speak to the prince in his chamber once more."

The princess agreed. Of course, she planned to have her servant give the prince a sleeping potion as she had done before. But that night when the prince went to bed, he asked the servant what the rustling in his room had been the night before. The servant confessed that he had been ordered to give the prince a sleeping potion, and that a distressed lady had visited him in his room.

"Tonight I am ordered to do it all again," the servant cried.

"Pour out the potion and place the empty cup by my bed," the prince instructed. "I will pretend to be asleep."

The servant did as the prince asked. When the lady entered his room the prince recognized her voice at once. It was his dear wife!

The prince sprang up, released from his enchantments. "At last I am truly free," he cried. "The evil princess put a spell on me so that I would forget you," he told his wife. "Now that I hear your voice, it has taken away my blindness."

Quickly, the lady and her love left the castle. They found the griffin waiting outside and seated themselves on its back. The griffin carried them over the Red Sea. When they came to the middle of the ocean, the lady dropped the nut that the north wind had given her. A tree sprang up through the waters and the griffin rested before taking them the rest of the way.

When they arrived home at last, they found their child had grown tall and lovely. They all lived happily together until the end of their days.

The Frog Prince

Retold after

The Brothers Grimm

IN olden times, when wishes came true, there lived a king whose daughters were all beautiful. The youngest daughter was so lovely that even the sun, who saw all things, was in awe when he shone upon her face.

Beside this king's palace was a shady forest. Inside that forest was a lime tree. And under that lime tree was a deep spring.

This was where, on hot days, the youngest princess liked to pass the time. When she tired of sitting and gazing into the cool, deep water, the princess played beside the spring with her golden ball. Throwing the ball high into the air and catching it was her favorite game, and she played it over and over again.

One day, the princess threw the ball so high into the air that it did not land in her outstretched hands. Instead it bounced upon the ground and rolled into the spring.

The princess ran to the edge of the water and watched the ball disappear, for the spring was so deep you could not see the bottom. Then the princess began to cry. She sobbed on and on.

It seemed the princess would never stop crying. Then a voice called out to her.

"Your crying would break a heart of stone. Tell me, what's the matter, Princess?"

The princess stopped weeping long enough to look and see who had spoken to her. In the spot the voice had come from she saw a frog poking his ugly head out of the water.

"I am crying for my golden ball. It has

fallen into the spring and is lost forever," the princess answered. "I would give all of my fine clothes and jewels — everything I have in the world — to have my ball back. But I don't know why I am telling you. You are nothing but a nasty green frog."

"Dry your eyes, Princess," the frog croaked. "I do not want your clothes or jewels. But perhaps you will promise to let me eat from your plate and drink from your cup. If I can sleep on your pillow and be your friend from now on, I will bring you your ball back."

"I promise!" the princess said, clapping her hands. Though really the princess had no intention of keeping her promise.

He's just a silly frog, she thought. *He can't leave the spring, and he could never be a friend to a princess!*

As soon as the princess made her promise, the frog dove deep down into the water. He was only gone a short while. When he appeared again he had the golden ball in his mouth. He tossed it onto the grass beside the princess.

As soon as the princess saw her ball, she picked it up and ran off with it.

"Wait!" the frog cried. "Take me with you! I can't keep up on my short green legs!"

But the princess did not stop. She ran all the way back to the castle without once thinking of the frog or the promise she'd made him.

The next evening, as the princess was sitting down to dinner, she heard a strange noise. *Flip-flap. Flip-flap.* It sounded like something flopping up the marble stairs. A moment later there was a light tap on the door. Then a voice sang out:

"Youngest daughter of the king,
open up and let me in.
Remember the promise that you made
by the spring in the forest shade."

The princess ran to open the door. When she saw the frog sitting there she was so frightened that she shut the door again quickly and returned to the table.

"Whatever is the matter?" the king asked his daughter, for he saw how flustered she was. "Who was at the door?"

"A nasty frog," the princess answered. "He fetched my ball from the spring yesterday when it fell in. In return I promised him that he could come and live with me and be my friend. But I never imagined he would come to the castle. Now he is here at the door and wants to come in!"

While she was speaking the frog knocked again and called out, louder than before:

"Youngest daughter of the king,
open up and let me in.
Remember the promise that you made
by the spring in the forest shade."

The king looked sternly at his daughter. "You have made a promise and you must keep it. Go and open the door for your guest."

So the princess opened the door and the little frog hopped over to the table.

"Please, lift me up so I can sit beside you," the frog said.

The princess hesitated until she saw the king's scowl. Then she quickly bent down and placed the wet little frog on the table.

"Please, push your plate closer so that I may eat from it, " the frog croaked.

Again, the princess hesitated. Then at last she pushed her plate close to the frog, who used his long sticky tongue to eat a large meal. The princess, however, had lost her appetite. She hardly ate anything at all. She was anxious to leave the table when the frog spoke again.

"Please, tip your cup for me so I may take a drink," he said.

The princess did as she was asked, but

she cringed when the frog's warty lips touched the rim of the cup.

"Now I'm tired," the frog said. "Please carry me to your bed and place me on your pillow."

Gingerly, the princess picked up the frog and carried him upstairs. She placed him beside her on a silken pillow. The little frog slept all night, while the princess tossed and turned.

The next morning, as soon as it was light, the frog woke up and hopped down the stairs and out of the castle.

"At last he is gone," the princess said. "I am rid of him forever."

But the princess was not rid of him. The frog returned the next night to sleep on her pillow. And again the next.

On the third night, the princess woke before the sunrise. She saw there was no frog on her pillow. Instead, standing at the foot of her bed was a handsome prince.

The prince looked at the princess with

the most beautiful eyes the girl had ever seen.

"Thank you," he said. "You have broken the cruel spell that was placed upon me by a bad fairy. I was forced to live in the body of a frog until a princess allowed me to sleep three nights on her pillow. You kept your promise and have left me with only one desire: that you will follow me back to my kingdom, be my bride, and let me love you for as long as you live."

The princess did not waste any time in answering. She had fallen in love with the prince the moment she laid eyes on him.

When the princess gave her consent and her father gave his, a splendid carriage pulled up to the castle. Eight milk-white horses were hitched to the front. Filled with joy, the couple set out for the prince's kingdom. There they lived long and happily together.